MW00916332

Acknowledgements

We would be remiss not to mention the enormous impact that great early childhood education has had on Estelle's development. While we have certainly nurtured Estelle's creative pursuits, she has had exceptional pre-school experiences at both the Westborough YWCA in central Massachusetts and the Harris School in southern New Hampshire. Her teachers have been amazing, and we are eternally grateful for their care and guidance over the years. Your efforts are reflected in the writing of this story.

First Printing, 2021

ISBN 978-1-7366674-0-8

**Published by Stena-Rose LLC
Produced by Rosemary Lopez
Send all inquiries to** contact@stenarose.com

The Pandas are sleeping, but they will be up soon. Today, they are having a pajama party!

The Pandas got out of bed to eat breakfast. Pop ate bamboo bake and her little sister, Lulu, had pancakes.

After breakfast, Pop and Lulu went for a walk in their neighborhood.

On the walk, they ran into their friend, the Giraffe, who said, "I'm going to your pajama party later."

They also ran into their lion friends who were going to the store to buy pajamas for the party.

Their bunny friends were hopping along in the town. They were also going to be at the pajama party.

As they passed the pijama shop, their dog friends were running into the store to get clothes for the party.

Pop and Lulu stopped at the Bamboo Shack for some bamboo treats, and talked to their horsey friends while they ate.

On the way home, Pop and Lulu stopped at the home of their unicorn friends to rest because the sun was really hot.

They took a nap on the hammocks because they were tired. Pandas like to take naps.

The pandas woke up and went back home to get ready for the party. The unicorns would join them later.

They got home and started cleaning and decorating. Lulu swept the floor while Pop hung streamers.

Some of the guests arrived. They went to the TV room to watch their favorite movie, "The Bunny Guard."

After the movie, they hung out and played games.

Lulu wanted to roast marshmallows, so they went outside to do just that while the unicorns caught fish.

They went inside to get ready for bed. The unicorns put on their facial masks in the bathroom while the bunnies and lions waited their turn.

Lulu, the parrot, the dogs, and giraffes brushed their teeth together in the bathroom.

Pop gathered everybody to read a bedtime story. Their friends sat quietly and listened to the story.

They all fell asleep and had a dream of a peaceful day together at the beach.

What should they do next?

ABOUT ESTELLE (the storyteller)

Estelle-Marie Camilus is a precocious first grader whose creativity and imagination are without bounds. She's an American-born girl of Haitian and Puerto Rican descent who literally spends every waking hour thinking about her next creation. As much as she likes to talk about, and dabble with, these ideas, Estelle also loves to party! She enjoys gatherings and sleepovers with family tremendously. Since she hasn't been able t o do much of that during the pandemic, she opted to write a story about it.

ABOUT BROOKLYNN (the artist)

Fort Wayne, Indiana based artist, Brooklynn Deane, has been perfecting her art skills for the past several years. At just eleven years old, Brooklynn's primary passion is pencil sketching. Aside from pencil art, Brooklynn loves to expand her knowledge by working with colored pencils, charcoal, and even digital art. Brooklynn loves creating original sketches of humans, animals, anime characters, and designing miniature30 home interior models. Brooklynn loves music and finds visual inspiration from some of her favorite musical artists such as BillieEilish & Melanie Martinez. In addition to the arts, Brooklynn has a passion for Japanese Culture. She studies Japanese language and looks forward to traveling to Japan in the near future. She is excited to delve into Japanese cuisine, lifestyle, and experience anime up-close and personal, to gain more artistic inspirations. At just eleven years old, Brooklynn started her own business to sell her artwork, Br Art, LLC. She launched her website in July 2020. She is excited to be able to share her art with the world.

You can find her artwork at www.BrArtStuff.com
Email Brooklynn at BrArtStuff@gmail.com
Follow Brooklynn at @BrArtStuff

Made in the USA
Las Vegas, NV
17 March 2021